FOR TESS AND FILIP.

And for all children with big dreams, or small ones. Don't give up hope,

because sometimes the most unlikely dreams come true.

An

FOR MEES.

Eline

First published in Belgium and Holland by Clavis Uitgeverij, Hasselt – Amsterdam, 2015
Copyright © 2015, Clavis Uitgeverij

English translation from the Dutch by Clavis Publishing Inc. New York
Copyright © 2016 for the English language edition: Clavis Publishing Inc. New York

Visit us on the web at www.clavisbooks.com

Dreaming of Mocha written by An Swerts and illustrated by Eline van Lindenhuizen
Original title: Dromen van Mokka
Translated from the Dutch by Clavis Publishing

ISBN 978-1-60537-294-5

This book was printed in August 2016 at Publikum d.o.o., Slavka Rodica 6, Belgrade, Serbia

First Edition
10 9 8 7 6 5 4 3 2 1

DREAMING OF MOCHA

AN SWERTS & ELINE VAN LINDENHUIZEN

Clavis

NEW YORK

Florence wants a dog.
It doesn't matter what kind of dog.

JUST
ANY DOG.

To take care of and to pet.
To run with and to play with.

If she gets a dog,
she will NEVER whine again
and ALWAYS be good.
That's what she promised Mom.

But Mom isn't so sure,
because dogs shed and
leave dirty paw prints.

And Dad has his doubts too,
because dogs like to dig
in his nice, neat garden.

And that's why Florence
still doesn't have a dog.

And that's also why she searches
every field and every park.

Because she hopes ONE DAY she will find one.

A homeless dog that no one wants.

WHY?

Because it is too fat. Or too thin.
Or too quiet. Or too wild. Or too this. Or too that.
But it doesn't matter to Florence.

As long as
IT'S A DOG

One day, when Florence has given up all hope
and is daydreaming on the swings with a bottle of juice,

she SUDDENLY sees a dog in the bushes.

In her own garden! And without an owner!

She stretches out her hand and the little dog immediately comes sniffing.

His messy brown fur hasn't seen a brush for ages.

But it's LOVE at first sight for Florence.

When Mom goes to wake Florence the next morning,
Florence is already up.
Nicely dressed and with her hair in pigtails.

"AREN'T YOU THE EARLY BIRD!"
Mom says, surprised.

Florence smiles and blows her a kiss.
At breakfast, Florence talks nonstop. About this and that.

But when Mom and Dad
aren't looking, she lets
pieces of sausage and
cheese slip into
her pockets.

After breakfast, Florence disappears to her room,
but a moment later she storms down the stairs again.
"I'LL BE OUTSIDE!" she calls to Mom in the kitchen.
"All right," Mom says.
Shortly afterwards, Mom walks through the hall with some laundry.

But what does she see there?
It looks like a tornado went by. And there are
muddy tracks everywhere... from little feet...
or are those little PAWS?

Mom follows
the tracks to
Florence's room.

She opens the door and Florence
looks STARTLED. "You look like you've
seen a ghost!" Mom laughs, but then she feels
something tickling her ankle.
She looks down and then she sees

A GHOST!
It's an extremely hairy ghost
that looks a lot like a dog!

"THIS IS MOCHA," Florence says softly,
pointing at the little tag on his collar.

"PLEASE, MOM, CAN I KEEP HIM?"

Mom can't believe her eyes. She is very upset.

"Let's... discuss this...
with Dad," she stammers.

Until they know who Mocha's owner is,
MOCHA can stay with Florence.

THEY HAVE THE TIME
OF THEIR LIVES.

They run through the garden.
Go hunting for bears.
Jump in the leaves.

Scare the neighbor's cat.
And lie down in the grass
or dig deep holes in the garden.

With MOCHA on
her lap, Florence dreams
of even more exciting
adventures.

Florence is as happy as can be,
but she is feeling a bit anxious too.
Because there are posters EVERYWHERE.
WITH MOCHA'S PICTURE
And underneath it in big letters: FOUND.
Plus a phone number. Mocha's owner will call soon enough.

That's what EVERYONE hopes.

EVERYONE?
  Well, everyone except Florence.
She hopes Mocha can stay with her forever.

  And that's why she brings a black pen
    whenever she takes Mocha for a walk.
  And then she changes the six of
  the phone number into an eight.
    Or she draws a moustache or
    a pair of glasses on Mocha's snout.

But one day **he** is at the door. WHO?
Yes, it's MOCHA'S owner. "I'm Leon," he says.

Mom offers him a cup of coffee. And Florence?

She is astonished, because Leon looks very different than she thought he would.

He's not a villain who scared Mocha away.

No, Leon is a sweet old man and Mocha jumps up and wags his tail when he sees him.

"BAD DOG! Running off by yourself looking for adventure!" Leon says.

But he is clearly not **really** upset,
because he smiles and strokes Mocha's fur.

Florence gets a funny
feeling in her stomach.
She really wants to be
happy for Mocha and Leon,
but she just can't.
She's going to miss
MOCHA!

Leon comes to visit often, as promised.

Florence is waiting anxiously long before they arrive.

And when they are almost at the house, Leon unleashes MOCHA.

Mocha sprints ahead until he lands in Florence's arms.

The reunion is always a happy one, but that's also
why saying goodbye is always so hard.

"SHALL WE GET A DOG TOO?" Mom suggests one day.

Dad nods enthusiastically and Leon's eyes sparkle.

But Florence shrugs and looks at the floor.

Deep down in her HEART she only wants Mocha.

But she doesn't want to say that, because she really likes Leon.

When Leon leaves with Mocha,
Florence watches them as usual
until they are no bigger
than two small dots.

But this time
THE DOTS
stop and turn around!

Maybe Leon forgot something,
Florence thinks. The next moment
Leon and MOCHA are back.
Leon has a big smile on his face.
   He knows Mocha likes
      being with Florence.
AND THAT IS WHY HE SOLEMNLY SAYS:
"If you promise to come
   and visit me often with Mocha,
      you can take care of him FOREVER."

Florence can't believe what she's hearing.
   "Forever?" she repeats.
      "YES," says Leon, loud and clear.

Florence's HEART jumps with joy.

"I PROMISE," she says.

And then again, but louder: "I PROMISE!"

And then again, but now so loud that the whole street can hear it

"I PROMISE!"

Her eyes sparkle and, with MOCHA
following close behind, she does a wild dance.

Leon shakes with laughter and wipes away a tear.
This is right, he thinks,
and goes home with a happy heart.